Henry O'Meara

Ballads of America and Other Poems

Henry O'Meara

Ballads of America and Other Poems

ISBN/EAN: 9783744788410

Printed in Europe, USA, Canada, Australia, Japan

Cover: Foto ©Andreas Hilbeck / pixelio.de

More available books at **www.hansebooks.com**

BALLADS OF AMERICA

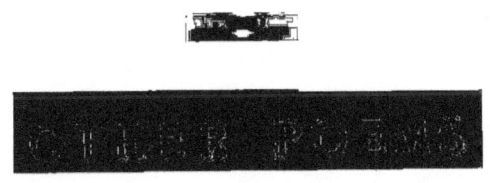

OTHER POEMS

HENRY O'MEARA

... et haec olim meminisse juvabit ...

BOSTON

PRELUSIVE.

IF prelusive prose annexed to proemial verse be not a vestibule too bold for this modestly proportioned volume, a line of acknowledgment here may be admissible. The hymns and songs cannot now be claimed as of first presentation, the former, with the musical compositions, having been produced from the press of Roeder, at Leipsic, and, with the latter, issued in the sheet-music form by an American house. It is grateful also to add an acknowledgment of the flattering comments and substantial guarantees received from gentlemen whose places in literature and public life would alone be sufficient to warrant this publication, and particularly of the kindly words and good wishes, as well as acceptance of a Dedication, from one whose name is in itself an adornment in this connection, — Dr. Oliver Wendell Holmes.

In regard to the groups of poems, it is perhaps timely to state that the two which may appear elliptical in theme are designed as nuclei of more systematic collections, — that under the title "Revolutionary Period" being projected for a series on events in chronological sequence which may be designated as the "Siege of Boston"; and that under "Shakespearian Pearls," for the portrayal of conceptions of the master dramatist which are not found suitable for stage delineation, or of such elements in the acted characters as are deemed too subtile for histrionic embodiment.

PREFACE TO THE SECOND EDITION.

THE first edition of the "Ballads of America" having been completely disposed of, and having been complimented with flattering words from something more than a hundred periodicals and recognized critics, including the world-prized poets John G. Whittier and Oliver Wendell Holmes, the author has felt warranted in sending forth a second. The plates of all the pages have been gone over with care for verbal and typographical improvements; and at the end of the Miscellaneous there have been added the fifteen new poems — from "A Life's Love Song" to the "Naval Ode" written for the City of Boston.

FROM OUR FOREMOST LIVING POETS.

THE author of "Ballads of America" has received the following from the two venerated survivors of the distinguished band of American poets whose lives and thoughts have been almost coeval with the century.

The names of John G. Whittier and Oliver Wendell Holmes are placed here simply in the order of seniority.

JOHN G. WHITTIER.

I have read with much satisfaction the spirited "Ballads of America." I like especially the "Coast Guard" and the tribute to John Boyle O'Reilly.

Truly thy friend,
JOHN G. WHITTIER.

Henry O'Meara, Boston.

OLIVER WENDELL HOLMES.

296 BEACON STREET, BOSTON,
May 25, 1891.

My Dear Mr. O'Méara : —

I am almost afraid to compliment you on your fresh and beautiful book after the flattering tribute you have paid me in your Dedication and in the poem especially inscribed to me. I must, however, thank you for the spirited and variously pleasing poems which come to me in a dress which commends them to my taste and makes the new volume a most welcome ornament to my book-table. I hope that you will live to give us many more songs of patriotism, friendship, and all the generous emotions which find their fitting expression in melodious verse.

Believe me, dear Mr. O'Meara,
Very truly and cordially yours,
OLIVER WENDELL HOLMES.

CONTENTS.

PROEMIAL.

A SAGE who gleaned from all things inly gain,
　　With test of load on load his pupil plied,
Till Labor's part came leagued with that of Pain —
" Enough," spoke he: " you've borne this grosser
　　strain —
　　Feel now the lesson's subtler weight beside :
Not by men's force alone is victory won —
　　Allied must fortitude and effort be,
Great deeds by strength with suffering joined are
　　done,
For dual ways of life merge these in one —
　　Through each there lies but variance of degree :
Doing and bearing blend in shaded line.
　　And high-lit power is reared on dim-wrought
　　base.
Low toils in tears suffused exalted shine.
Achievements on endurance shaped define
　　A free land's course — the road that lifts a race."

Take the sweet poetry of life away

And what remains behind?

WORDSWORTH.

REVOLUTIONARY PERIOD

Things of deep sense we may in
   prose unfold,
But they much more in lofty
   numbers told.

WALLER.

THE BOSTON MASSACRE.

MARCH 5, 1770.

'TIS March — the frosted ways are crystal
'neath the crescent light,
Fitly relucent glow for deeds that blot, yet gild
this night —
Its stain, the patriots' mantling blood as light
effused as spray,
Its gold, an auric glimmer ere a dawning Nation's
day,
Rising to flame in freemen's souls, hot-fanned
by hirelings' breath,
While air bereft of liberty is charged with dews
of death.

Long has a People's Chivalry hurled back the
    helot chain,

Spurned links of thrall with proud will fetter-
    less in vain;

A Charter scorned, an om'nous squadron brood-
    ing on the Bay,

Troops quartered on a chafing Town tell Britain's
    lust of sway.

With idolled leaders outlawed — imposts and
    vassal taxes planned —

Her aliened offspring yield no tribute of a filial
    hand.

" Adams and Hancock will be seized ! " — this
    night the warnings ring —

Through King Street rumors steal despite the
    sentry of the King —

" Disperse, conspirators ! " the stern demand is
    heard from him —

The group, in sullen silence firm, is riveted and
    grim ;

Hence free civilians throng, here Preston's rein-
forcements meet —

A moment, and a deathlike stillness falls upon
the street.

Fiercely the scene is rent with roar of musketry
and strife —

Swiftly the startled people wake to patriotic life :

Boston is roused to hear her stricken sons'
avenging cry,

The crimson on her streets, foreshowing crime of
deeper dye.

Hearts beat — " to arms " — eyes flash like signal
fires on Beacon Height,

New England's righteous flame is stirred to rage
of martial might ;

" Fire ! Fire ! " rings forth — from Brattle Street's
bold tower outpeals the bell —

That fire ignites a Nation's life — that peal is
thraldom's knell.

Then was a blow at king-craft by a sovereign
   people aimed —
Then, as an Adams proved, " an Empire's sever-
   ance stood proclaimed."

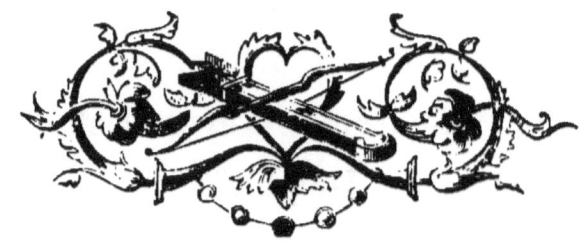

SAM ADAMS.

SONNET ON THE WHITNEY STATUE, BOSTON.

LEADER by Nature sent to stir an age
　　When men were kindled with the pent-up ire
　That rebel son had caught from burning
　　sire —
Hero whose prescient thought and theme presage
The later franchise on our Nation's page ;
　Whose swerveless powers new chivalry inspire.
　This bronze outbreathes an innate spirit fire,
Bespeaks a statesman brave, a patriot sage,
　A mind of adamant to mould the time —
Betokens olden Boston's worth and fame,
　Tells that a People's flash of hope sublime
Is fanned by Genius into Freedom's flame,
　That still four generations' deeds and prime
Are stamped and pictured in the Adams' name.

THE BATTLE OF SHIRLEY STRAIT.

BOSTON HARBOR, 1776.

IN Boston's Spring of Pride — her soil from
    sentinel ranks set free —
While Britain's navy yet unvanquished shut her
    from the sea,
King George's vulpine brood of ships hung still in
    hostile quest,
Their black hulls marred, as blots on Liberty, her
    Harbor's breast,
Spread like a low'ring brow of war across the
    Bay —
Nantasket's surf-wrought crescent spanned to
    Winthrop's wall of spray.

"I'll vow," the British captain said, "no rebel
    privateer
Shall dare to leave this Town or stir a sail while
    we lie here."

They dreamt not of the sturdy hearts with whom
    their fleet should cope,
Of Mugford's men whose fishing-smack bore off
    their navy's " Hope."
Now with the " Franklin " steals the fisher hero
    forth to·Shirley Strait —
The saucy cruiser " Lady Washington " a worthy
    mate ;
But here capricious tides and currents lure his
    hast'ning band,
And craft that scorned a navy's strength lie
    captured by the strand.
With Britain's instinct to surprise the trapped
    or supine prey,
An armed flotilla from the fleet speeds proudly
    to the fray ;
Barges and boats in shoals careen around th'
    encircled prize —
But stay — the soul of Battle blazes in the pa-
    triots' eyes !

Though tier-shot sweep their spar and shroud,
    and langrage tear their sail,

From cannons' mouths they hurl back musket-
 balls like death-borne hail;
Wheeling, the barges meet at every turn in that
 swift eddy
The " Franklin's " levelled metal and the swivels
 of the " Lady."
" One effort more — quick — board their decks ! "
 the British leader cries —
Grappling and scrambling from their boats, the
 agile seamen rise;
" Lively, my men," — calls Mugford; " pikemen,
 show your mettle now ! " —
The foes impetuous scale the boarding-net from
 stern to bow;
Defenders and assailants lock in fierce palestric
 strife
As, man to man, each grimly fronts the struggle
 of a life.

The sun that early lit the fight grows lurid ere
 its set,
And looks askant o'er Shawmut's hills to find
 them struggling yet.

At last with spear and pike-head all that blood-
stained net is rent,

The boldest barges crippled, the heart's-tide of
the tenants spent.

Sullen the proud flotilla turns to leave its prize
unwon,

Its stately sortie foiled, its vaunted task un-
done.

. . . .

When dawn shone over Winthrop Head a child
by Shirley's tide

Discerned the British leader's form, a spear-
wound in the side;

But dearly was that victory for a striving
people bought.

For Mugford's last long cruise was done — his
final battle fought;

No more his feats would thrill old Marblehead —
her captain brave

Had found the death he courted in that duel of
the wave.

IN MEMORY OF MARY WASHINGTON.

THE OBELISK DESIGNED A HALF CENTURY AGO FOR THE GRAVE OF WASHINGTON'S MOTHER IS STILL UNFINISHED AND NEGLECTED.

NOW are the centenary days unrolled,
    On whose swift round a Nation's theme
      is told —
Our Chieftain chosen with a land's acclaim,
With civic wreath encircling martial fame —
In fealty our love's deep proffer made,
Our debt to Washington in flushed hearts paid.
But while that name, in life renascent reigns,
One duty lives — one echoing void remains.

In shadow of Virginia's valley dim,
Where she was wont to muse — to dream of
    him,

Lies low the heart that all his pulsing shared,
Throbbed in his hopes, in pains and perils
    dared ; —
The mother, whose unnoted scenes were done
When far-off pæans were sounding for the son.
A hundred Springs have waked the glad'ning
    ground,
And Autumns thrown their radiant cinctures
    round ;
Yet we, insensate, yield not fruitful care,
While winds have planted weeds and wild
    flowers there.

O, heirs of him, bequeathed a ransomed Land,
Repay that life's rich meed with filial hand ;
No more remiss in memory of the dead,
Who sleeps by lonely Rappahannock's Bed ;
Set forth the Obelisk of a century's thought —
Redeem that Vale where War's red deeds were
    wrought ;
Let brothers' blood that full her soil baptized,
Blent in her mound, be fused and crystallized ;

Deep in her shrine amid the meadows sere,
In living lines serene as her, and clear,
Chisel that word above the chastened breast,
With shining love reluming shrouded rest —
" Mary, Mother of our Washington, lies here ! "

CIVIL WAR PERIOD

For rudest minds with harmony
were caught,
And civil life was by the Muses
taught.

ROSCOMMON.

THE MARTYR LIBERATOR.

ON UNVEILING THE EMANCIPATION GROUP, "LINCOLN STRIKING
THE SHACKLES FROM SLAVES."

LIFT up the group — lift him who raised the
    lowly of his kind,
Friend of the slave — who struck the shackles
    from the limbs and mind;
Embalm in bronze a Nation's loss — a People's
    guardian slain —
The freedman's shattered Shield — embody, too,
    a Race's gain!

Lift high the life-linked forms — they cannot
    reach his lofty thought;
Make firm — they never can outlive the fame
    and work he wrought.

Yet shroud no more his lineaments — nor dwell
    on loss alone,
The death was but his country's grief — its
    grandeur's still his own.
Not all the groups of gods in Attic art or
    Antique story
Give bonds in brass of grander worth — more
    bright, emblazoned glory.

The lowliest flower, 'tis said, will sing to listen-
    ing ears that learn —
Nature shows rich analogies to those who will
    discern ;
Thus, too, this new Memorial speaks through
    voiceless bronze and stone —
Its sound is that of snapping chords, like Mem-
    non's wondrous tone ;
It tells of him to whom the call was given to
    see the right,
To speak the potent word and marshal men in
    Conscience might.

As when the moon, full crimson, peers through
    forest dense and dim,
And circumfusing, manifests each dark and
    knotted limb,
That lurid theme of war and slavery, death and
    lavished tears,
Kindles to sight the shame and sorrow of two
    hundred years.
Deep in the background of those darkly omened,
    bygone times,
The diorama shows two freighted barks from
    sundered climes, —
One bears to Plymouth men demanding free-
    dom of the soul,
One to Virginia wretches in the slaver's grim
    control.
Not all our picturing words nor lum'ning Art can
    show
The blight and suffering brought in that Dutch
    slave-ship's freight of woe.
Then first the Valley of the James resorbed the
    bondsman's breath —
Mother of States and Presidents, — she bore the
    germs of death.

But who can gauge the rain of tears and
   heart-wrung griefs that fell —
The wrongs and groans that rang since then
   what tongue of ire shall tell?
At last rose one who dared to do the martyr
   patriot part,
To warm deductions of the brain with prompt-
   ings of the heart —
The word of Science tells us that the heart force
   of a life
Would wear to dust a granite column grated
   by its strife;
And so the heart of Lincoln and the Nation
   blent as one,
Ground on the rock of Slavery till all its base
   was gone.
As brave Telemachus amid Honorius' victims ran,
He gave himself to dust that man might cease
   to trample man.
Furious arose the enslaving throng, and rang
   Secession's cry —
They rushed to arms lest Freedom live — he
   met them lest it die.

Occasions of great pith and moment, if they
    serve at all,

Like Manna of the Hebrews, must be gathered
    as they fall.

"Delenda est Carthago" was the shibboleth of old,

"Delenda est Servitus," later, grander deeds
    foretold ;

Stern L'Overture, on San Domingo's blood-
    drenched shore

A half a million in his land from Spanish bondage
    tore ;

But Lincoln gave four millions of a misprized
    race release,

Yet held to foes the waiting hands of union
    and of peace.

Forgiving then he met the conflict's brunt, the
    treason's scar,

As sandal copse bestowing perfume on the blades
    that mar ;

And like the sandal tree, his nature spurned a
    crawling thing —

Aspiring heart, as gentle blood, true chivalry
    should bring.

Swiftly the weapon of the assassin smote his startled brain.

Awe-struck the Nation heard her guide and cherished chief was slain;

Pulses then beat as one — a spray of tears bedewed the Land,

For him who held a People's hope and purpose in his hand.

Still, like a stream through snowy moon-lit fields,

His heart's effusive tide, a glowing, melting moisture yields.

His memory's sweet as winds that woo the white anemones —

His dying moan in blanched hearts wakes undying monodies.

    .   .   .   .

Round him, as Washington, the clustering stars of Union gather.

On him they fling the lustre of the Nation's head and father;

The first bequeathed their realm and rights to
    colonists oppressed.

The last redeemed a race, the wrongs of centu-
    ries redressed.

His temples' gory glow the laurels of his fame
    shall screen.

Like aloes that each hundredth year shall find
    alive and green.

Confide no more alone to cenotaphs or columns cold,

The cause — the memories that warm and wake-
    ful hearts should hold.

A thousand years agone, Dutch bulwarks checked
    the Zuyder Zee —

A thousand years to come must clay and wil-
    low curb that sea.

" The god of Nature sleeps," the pliant Epicurus
    taught :

" By wary work," cried saged Demosthenes, " our
    Freedom's bought."

Thus shall be stamped upon that broad based
    mound, a million graves —

" The martyr land of Lincoln ne'er again shall
    nurture slaves."

A race set free, the land at peace, his life and
    labor past, —

His euthanasia crowned, is crystallized in death
    at last ;

Ages of thraldom now with Lincoln's deedful
    days are done ;

The age of thronging thought and thronéd lib-
    erty begun !

MEMORIALS ON GETTYSBURG FIELD.

THERE let memorials deathless rise to tell
    Each spot where martyrs to their prized
        land fell,
Each monolith of praise — of martial meed,
Standing 'mid light of monumental deed,
Where heroes dared — their lives last proffer
    made,
Their measure full in immolation paid.

Not dead lie these dumb symbols of the strife,
But mutely speaking that most crucial life,
That struggle of a Nation's heart sustained
When patriot nerves were tense and pulsing
    strained.

When Union vital hung upon the field,
And listened for the import it should yield —
On Gettysburg, where centred foes were hurled
With clash of impact echoing to the world!

RONDEAU ON U. S. GRANT.

O CHIEFTAIN gone! Your vital deeds
remain,
Though stilled be vibrant pulse and war-stirred
brain.
Hushed be the heart — the living spirit flown —
Our Union cleaves to your bond as her own —
Claims with a deathless grasp your life-wrought
chain
Though past and crowned be internecine pain.
Its lingering impulse still her sons retain —
Into our lives has yours, great leader grown,
O Chieftain gone!
Ever our memories glow your fire maintain,
Enkindling patriot potency again —
Never shall men, while name of Grant be
known,
Despair of martial voice, of hero tone —
Invoke, O vanished chief, your spell in vain,
O Chieftain gone!

THE HERALD OF THE NEW SOUTH.

WRITTEN FOR THE MEMORIAL TO HENRY WOODFEN GRADY, ATLANTA, GA.

MUST we concede the life so swiftly flown
    That seemed but yesterday to breathe
      our own —
The pulsing stayed that through our lands he
    sent,
In whose one impact North and South were
    blent —
His cords, yet vital, stilled with tone abound-
    ing —
His heartstrings sundered by their vibrant
    sounding?

Too well we feel the import of our fears,
The wide-flashed word, "The South is steeped
    in tears."
Fitly she weeps for her chivalric son
Who turned to her, in flush of triumph won,

The filial voice to gain her glad applause —
The golden tongue to plead — to gild her
    cause.

That spirit note — the music of his speech,
Is silenced now in earthly hearings reach;
Snapped is the silvern thread — the resonant
    soul —
Though severed, still its pæans reverberant
    roll —
All hearts their hope-rung chants in mourning
    merge.
All joyous dreams translate into a dirge.

Fallen in hero prime of conscious power,
His fame lives on and soothes her anguished
    hour;
Yields to the land of Calhoun and of Clay
His name as heirloom to her later day —
A legacy by life's oblation left,
A breathing solace to a home bereft.

That knightly nature's gift — that intellect's
    grace,
Relieved attrition wrought by clash of race
That reason poised in sympathy supreme,
Revealed translucent pathos in his theme,
Bade clamor cease — taught candor's part to
    cure —
Bade truth appear more true, pure thought
    more pure.

But is the zenith reached — his record done,
His duty closed beneath meridian sun?
Was it for him like meteor flash to sweep —
Athwart the heavens, as vaulting lightnings
    leap
On living errand our dimmed orbit cleave —
On mission radiate, yet no message leave?

Ah, no — his flame rose not to fall anon —
His words as phrase to glitter and be gone;
Not evanescent in the minds of men,
His ling'ring oratory speaks again —

An era's nuncio in a nation's view —
An envoy of another South, and new.
For now through prescience 'neath his Southern
    skies
The grander vision greets our Northern eyes:
The proud mirage he conjured up we see —
His picturing of her potency to be,
Her virile wealth of sun and soil and ore
Her new-born freedom's force far nobler store.

With sectional lines and marring feuds effaced.
Their   racial   problems   solved — their   blots
    erased —
Full in that vision circumfused shall rise
A symbol that his life rays crystallize,
For all our state loves lit in him to stand —
For bonds that Georgia's genius lent to all our
    land.

VETERANS' RALLYING SONG.

NATIONAL ENCAMPMENT, G.A.R., BOSTON, 1890.

(Air—"*Marching through Georgia.*")

RALLY now in veteran lines at Victory's
    note of pride —
Life's truceless foe is striking laurelled heroes
    from our side,
Bid the bygone ranks return — their deeds with
    us abide —
    For we were Soldiers of Freedom!

Chorus.

Hurrah! Hurrah! send forth a sound of cheer!
Hurrah! Hurrah! for comrades far or near —
Rally as in days when none could heed a doubt
    or fear —
    For we were Soldiers of Freedom!

Let our risen armies move along the gloried
way —
Our war-spent legions live again in patriots'
glad array,
Marshalled by remembrance dear aroused in us
to-day —
　For we were Soldiers of Freedom!

Chorus, etc.

May our camp-fire's glow relume the memories
they bore,
And voices that revive the bivouac's cheer —
the battle's roar,
Sing the praise of peace and union blended
evermore —
　For we were Soldiers of Freedom!

Chorus, etc.

LATER THEMES

The world is so grand and so inexhaustible that themes for poems should never be wanting.

GOETHE.

ILLUMINED LIBERTY.

AT DEDICATION OF THE STATUE OF LIBERTY, NEW YORK.

NOT as a gift inert to stand
   Or alien at this haven view,
But guest in glow of Lafayette's land,
Traversing space his heart-reach spanned —
   An old World's envoy to a New —

Not with the blaze that Furies' eyes,
   In France's Night of Terror bore,
But with rays to fuse the Nations' skies —
Genius of Freedom radiant rise,
   A halo round our symbolled shore!

Point to their course the people's weal,
   Republics charged with Manhood's freight,
Show reefs that social mists conceal —
'Mid rocks of Anarchy reveal
   Each wreck that marks an omened fate.

Flash out electric ire to awe
   The foes that low'r on chartered Light,
Dream that our Nation's prophets saw —
Liberty sphered in lucent law,
   In anadem of aureoled Right!

JOHN HARVARD'S MEMORIAL.

BY Time entombed, untraced by living eye —
   Oblivion-merged his vital embers lie,
Whose primal spark, the glow of Harvard's
   name,
Enkindled first New England Culture's flame;
Still shines his soul's expression crystallized,
Through loving care of Art idealized
His lumined form in speaking bronze revealed,
His spirit clear in lineaments unsealed.

Not all the radiance shed o'er Pharos Isle
That beaconed far the gateway of the Nile
Outshone the wide-sent rays of him revered,
In form ideal on this "delta" reared.
At morn's tint Memnon from his verberant
   shrine
Evoked sweet tones, to faith of old divine:

This Life, of new-dawned science prescient long,
Tuned forth our learning, poesy, and song.

Full in its beams Memorials rose to tell
Of heroes that in Manhood's morning fell,
Chivalric sons who proffered sword and pen—
Who burned to strive or die to ransom men,
With gift that scholarship aglow can yield,
With martial flash to light a "Soldier's Field,"
To fuse a realm — recast a people free —
Their fire was caught, fair Harvard, all from
        thee!

BENJAMIN P. SHILLABER.

"MRS. PARTINGTON."

THE spirits, full oft, that in Fancy abide,
 Show briars 'neath the blossoms of wit that
  adorn,
And hearts that in roses of humor confide
Are pierced with asperity's barb which they
 hide —
 Transfixed on their path with adversity's
  thorn.

This mind that found root in the mirth-
 planted bower
 Where nettles in touch with soft petals
  appear,
Turned to view but the bloom of a ripe nature's
 dower —
A genius of kindliness radiant in flower,
 With calyx of wit and corolla of cheer.

Good-by to his life-growths and loved themes
    they bring —
To the pathos and pleasantry conjured alike,
Whose genial conceits to fond memories cling,
As his verse bore no venom and satire no
    sting —
Good-by, Mrs. Partington, Blifkins, and Ike!

A GREETING TO GLADSTONE.

STATESMAN, whose pæans have sounded
    out fourscore,
Accept a greeting from our echoing shore —
Approach the twentieth century's portico
With steps that never senile lapse foreshow —
For now upon this opened eightieth year,
With virile cause and firm advanced career,
A continent may not contain your name,
Nor ocean's bound confine your buoyant fame.
Grand oak that spreads with ever-strengthening
    form —
That grows and towers through strivings and
    through storm —
Your boughs all people's aspirations span,
All hopes uphold that reach the rights of
    man —
Your sprays their sundered works for freedom
    bind
With sympathies and oratory twined.

Still in the roll of deeds for manhood done —
The record of those moral victories won —
In rounded life of thought for all the race,
Our partial eyes perceive one interspace —
'Mid strifes with vested wrong — with racial
    woe —
We see you in remote horizon low;
Turn now from themes of home or Orient far,
Meet once the Western trend of empire's Star —
Visit this soil with trans-Atlantic rays
Whose proud autonomy evokes your praise;
Come as a meteor at meridian height
That arches lands with eloquence of light —
The century shall not mark a nobler meeting —
Columbia claims to speak this life's autumnal
    greeting.

BOSTON TO MARIETTA.

ON THE OHIO CENTENNIAL.

FAIR daughter seated by Ohio's stream,
　　First offspring of the East in virile days
The rugged West to win and then redeem,
May not our thought sound now a mother's theme,
　　Maternal throbs attune thy century's lays?

May vibrant memories of these years unite
　　To speak the kinship of our parted band
That reared thy radiant Commonwealth in light,
In love for law, for knowledge, freedom, right —
　　For all that chartered ground where Boston's
　　children stand.

THE HERO COAST GUARD.

DEDICATED TO CAPTAIN JAMES AND THE LIFE-SAVERS AT NANTASKET.

" ANOTHER wreck upon the rocks!" —
        the sharp cry seemed a knell
That cleft the storm, and on the ears of toil-
        spent surfmen fell:
All night a captain valorous and a voluntary
        crew
Swerveless had fought the sea — and now their
        summons comes anew.

Thrice from the wrath of waves they wrest
        lorn ships and freights of lives —
At weary dawn this call from dread Atlantic
        Reefs arrives.
On Stony Beach, on fissured bluff, they speed
        their desperate way,
With boat and buoy through blinding sleet-gusts
        and disputing spray.

Now they descry the sufferers in the shrouds,
    but know not pause —
A ship lies crushed on boulders in that ledge's
    cruel jaws.

" Quick — push the lifeboat off ! "   " It can't live
    here," a follower cries ;
" It must — those men aloft must live," the
    leader wroth replies ;
The Hunt-gun's hope-charged missile spans the
    bow — the hawser's fast —
" Good ! — swing the breeches-buoy ! " a saving
    link is clutched at last.
" 'Tis vain — the whip-line is entangled in the
    wreckage there ! "
On ship and shore a sense of fate is settling to
    despair ;

" Yet see ! " a fisher's smack, unawed by what
    those scenes forbode,
Manned by three dauntless souls, athwart the
    raging maelstrom rowed.

"They're lost!" the captain moans — "but where
     that fragile craft has been
Should we not be, aboard the sturdiest boat this
     coast has seen?"
Answering with oars they near the ship despite
     the angered main,
Nor flinch, though baffling breakers fling them
     back again.

A struggling hour of noble onset waged for
     pendant life —
A firm-held place abreast the mainmast ends the
     awful strife.
Now, through that nest of death beneath the
     half-furled sail,
One figure moves from toppling mizzen safe to
     trembling rail.
His comrades follow, and 'mid cheers are brought
     to joyous reach;
The rescuers and rescued, all are borne along
     the beach.

But ah! not all — never can pleasure come from
    aught complete.

What form is that, the piteous, white face
    pleading in the sheet?

A young wife clam'rous cries, "My husband's
    saved? Speak — where is he?

Why have you left one man alone? O, point
    him now to me!"

Nerved where stern danger calls, unnerved their
    hearts where anguish crowds,

The heroes, wordless, show her that man lashed
    amid the shrouds.

.   .   .   .

Praise to these oaric knights while rocks be-
    speak their record won,

Their deeds of new-wrought chivalry, of un-
    priced duty done!

Perils by land and sea are shared, each search-
    ing Valor's core —

Their courage as their calling binds the ocean
    and the shore.

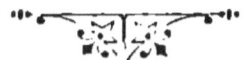

WELCOME TO THE WHITE FLEET.

WRITTEN FOR RECEPTION TO ADMIRAL WALKER AND OFFICERS
FROM THE SQUADRON OF EVOLUTION.

FLOWER of the fleet, of youngest bloom and
    best —
White group of sisters on our Harbor's breast,
Borne by the land's new wealth of fashioning
    skill,
By affluent forces of her 'wakening will —
Old Boston bids you welcome where abides
The halo round our home of " Ironsides ";
To you her fame-lit years a charge transfers —
A blazoned century's life be yours, as hers.

Turn filial here to find maternal greeting,
As turned our country's chief, his mission meet-
    ing —

Here first an infant craft essayed to cope
With Britain's bulk, to smite her navy's
    " Hope ";
Twin cruisers through the hull-walls tore a
    path,
Hurled back their langrage and their tier-shots'
    wrath;
Here where her fleet was banished from the
    Bay.
Low'ring like Fiends of War with lust of
    sway,
Our ocean envoys to an Old World's view,
Take now this parting tribute from the New.

Not at imperial beck from peasants wrung,
But out the spirit of a people sprung,
Your dower of strength our liberties attest —
The genius of this Giant in the West.
" Chicago," with the flag assigned to you
Uphold her pride who lights our vast Lake's
    view;

Colleague that bears for us a closer claim,
Set forth our City's honor with her name;
Patrons of both the lesson brave inspire
Fearless, as you, to meet the stress of fire;
Stand, "Yorktown," for our war of birthright past;
"Atlanta," speak for triumph in the last
And join with these in "marching to the sea,"
While "Boston" links the record of the three.

Go forth, bright Argosy, with theme un-
    rolled —
The banner with the stars increased threefold.
    At home, from some familiar height,
        But out no lofty meaning raised,
Our blaze of stars with streaks of light —
Ignobly placed to lure men's sight,
    Hangs oft unheeded and unpraised:
But when serene, alone, it shines,
    A joy on far ungenial lands,
Our wanderer — in its flaming lines —
The freeman's oriflamme divines —
    The people's might, for which it stands;

And there, against a foreign sky,
   Exulting scans its form unfurled —
There feels our symbolled Freedom nigh,
Resorbs her breath that bids it fly —
   Exalts in love her emblem o'er the world!

THE FLAG ABOVE THE SCHOOL.

UNFURL our emblem free —
   A star-lit bond to be —
  Our symbolled Love ;
May every ray abide,
A glory, as a guide,
Our Learning's course beside,
   And flame above.

There let its impulse glow,
Each line glad lessons show
   That youth may learn ;
Clear in their beams combined,
In league of stars divined —
Freedom in Union twined
   May all discern.

Banner whose sign we sing,
Whose themes proud visions bring,
    We hail thee now;
With peerless past in view,
Proffer a future true,
And loyal ties renew
    With free souls' vow!

DRAMATIC

Much is the force of heaven-bred poesy.

SHAKESPEARE.

SHAKESPEARIAN PEARLS.

—

ISABELLA — IN "MEASURE FOR MEASURE."

EXALTED issue of our Shakespeare's dream,
   Shine, Isabella, Star of cloistral roll —
The shadowed lot thy vows of life redeem
Is lit with radiance from a vestal beam —
   An effluent lustre out thy virgin soul!

.

Clad with thy vesture of illumined clay
   That Nature and Religion blent endow
To fire men's hearts, yet guilt-wrought heat
    allay,
With psychic charms too subtile for decay —
   Before thy power their tyrant passions bow.

IMOGEN — IN " CYMBELINE."

IN Imogen all pearls of wifehood shine,
  Conjugal truth and immolation lend
A life-lit halo to the spousal shrine
While Nature's gems in nuptial beams combine
  Where jewels of connubial lustre blend.

Clasped to this shrine, her wronged heart bides
    alone —
  Each radial impulse cleft by Love's recision —
Conjures an aureole phasma all her own,
A soul's perfusion as a nimbus thrown
  On her the centred angel of the vision.

CORDELIA — IN "KING LEAR."

FORMED by that Master's subtile flame and
 power,
 Creature most pure by crucial wrong refined,
Cordelia claims alone the precious dower —
The twin-born graces of a dual flower,
 Conjugal faith and filial ties entwined.

Ophelia pensive, Portia wise and fair,
 Juliet forlorn, Beatrice unbelieving.
Helena tried, Hermione true and rare —
Jewels you all creative genius share,
 But gemmed Cordelia is his soul's conceiving.

Though fond and fierce by turn be fickle Lear,
 She still untired in love, by fear unstirred,
Teaches to prize the simple and sincere —
To pierce the guise of Vanity's veneer,
 To scorn pretence and hate the hollow word.

Goneril vows and Regan bends to gain,
  Yet calm Cordelia clings to truth unswerving,
As innate trust and worth her heart sustain —
Self-poised above these sisters' sordid plane,
  Content and tranquil simply in deserving.

Peerless Cordelia, whose sweet Nature glows,
  A petalled-pearl of rose-embosomed dew,
That fresh fulfilment, not dry promise, shows —
As liquid benison e'er limpid flows,
  A guile-parched world's athirst for such as you!

HARRY MURDOCH.[1]

" Behold — as may unworthiness define — a little touch of Harry."
Shakespeare, " Henry V."

BOSTON yet looks on one bereavement —
    one link with Brooklyn's woe,
A loss that meets not Time's retrievement — a
    grief that will not go;
Impatient Death, with fiery breath, brushed off
    a loved life's bloom,
Shrivelled its blossoming hopes, and swept them
    down the hopeless tomb.

Of all who felt that fiendlike flame, that clutch
    of cruel Fate,
None leaves a more endearing name, none hearts
    more desolate,

[1] Burned at Brooklyn Theatre when in the rôle of " Pierre " in the
" Two Orphans."

Than we who mourn, untimely torn from work
of fame begun,
Our Harry Murdoch, genial Art and giftful
Nature's son.

Now round his memory trooping come hosts of
vanished friends —
There poor " Pierre " limps, slowly drooping —
here bold " Laertes " bends ;
Sad, hand in hand, " Our Boys " return, but
wit no more beguiles,
" Antony " sings no more, and " Diedrich "
brings but tearful smiles.

O Winds that fanned Doom's vengeful flame,
now moan for him you killed.
Waft our warm sorrow, with his fame, to home
and hearts now chilled ;
With swift simoon of sympathy our praise, our
comfort carry.
And cry with Shakespeare — " Lord in Heaven
bless thee, noble Harry ! "

REOPENING OF THE BOSTON MUSEUM.

HOME of gay Thalia! greeting wide the view
    Where column, stage, and fretted arch
    combine,
As touched by fairy wand — bedecked anew
  To grace loved Comedy's fair Columbine;
Like wanderer, with commingling smiles and
    tears,
  Who turns to scan his field of bygone dreams,
We, lingering, note how every scene endears—
  E'en barren parts bear mellow Memory's
    themes!

Here Smith and Keach bequeathed a generous
    soil,
   Here nightly gleamed the Thespian glow-
    worm's spark,
Ripe merit meeting histrionic toil,
   Where reaped a Barrett, Barron, Vincent,
    Clarke.
Time's change to rue — the favored Past to
    cite,
   Befits old friends, of cherished joys bereft;
Yet may we warrant all the present right
   While long our blithe, perennial Warren's
    left.[1]

---

[1] The last line is left unaltered, as the poem is to be regarded only in
connection with the time of the event for which it was written.

TO LAWRENCE BARRETT.

SEER of that chanted Art our nature craves
   To limn in light enshrouded days and men,
To echo deeds from dim Nirvana's caves —
Lift to new fame oblivion-lapsing graves —
   Vest their dead themes with vivid life again:
Hispanian, Moor, Venetian, sweep along —
   Speak in your fire — your histrion pulsing
     own —
The Dane tells dreamily his brooding wrong.
The hate-wrought Roman hisses in the throng —
   Loved Man o' Airlie croons his lullaby alone.

FLORAL

I would I had some flowers o' the
    spring that might
Become your time o' day; daffodils,
That come before the swallow
    dares; violets dim,
But sweeter than the lids of
    June's eyes,
Or Cytherea's breath.

WINTER'S TALE.

THE SPRING BULBS' ADVENT.

NOW from their chrysalis trance our bulb-
loves peer
From brumal bound unprisoned to assume
The hues that speak their forms' penumbra
near —
Nigh crystalled prime of this new flower-lit
year
Whose tints the prisms of the spring illume.

Here Tulip-cups cheer Flora's advent hours,
Sad Hyacinths bear Apollo's symbolled plaint,
Self-plumed Narcissi vaunt florescent powers—
Join Daffodils, Jonquils — all akin in flowers —
While vernal fingers fresh their petals paint.

Lone Colchicums their plighted leafage show
  As earnest of the bloom in autumn shed —
But lily vestals, reflex of the 'parted snow,
Prescient reveal their Resurrection glow —
  A halo gleaming round each aureoled head.

Thus souls resurgent in supernal guise,
  As bulbs, to life of loftier being cling:
From   earth-clad   germ   to   sun-rayed   growth
    arise —
Gazing relumed, intent upon the skies —
  Unfading flower in sempiternal Spring!

A PRECOCIOUS HYACINTH.

[The classic conceit as to the origin of the Hyacinth was that Apollo raised it from the blood of his beloved Hyacinthus, as a memorial to that victim of the envious Zephyrus.]

HAS Spring advanced, else why her envoys
     here —
These nuncios of bloom proclaiming nigh
Her matin primal in the bloss'ming year —
Coyly her bulbs from beds unfrosted peer,
    The coquette, Hyacinth, tempting Boreas' sky?

Too swift this herald spurns her season's speed —
    The sphere wherein her Vernal kin aspire.
Yet fit disowns a taint of Winter's breed —
Scion of stock so fair — so pure of seed,
    Was never offspring of Hibernal Sire.

Why seek to rise when no sweet colleague can,
    To greet thy suitors ere they sanguine call —
A pretty marplot in the flow'ring plan,
Outstepping Flora's ranks to win the van —
    To lead them captive in thy luring thrall?

Dost thou dispute the Storm-king's sway,
  In sortie plant the standard of the spring,
Or, self-doomed as Telemachus, essay
The conflict of fierce elements to stay —
  Athwart their strifes thy fragile body fling?

Ah! subtler forces draw thee thus apace
  To ope thy charms despite the boreal breath,
Frail nymph enamored of thy sun-god's face,
Oblivious of the fate that limned thy race
  The deed that wrought fond Hyacinthus' death.

Thy parent stem was reared, as poets sang,
  Apollo's grief to symbol yet assuage —
To speak his stricken love — allay his pang;
Flushed with that beauteous Spartan's blood she
    sprang
  Formed of that martyr to Zephyrus' rage.

Firstling of the bulb-queen's progeny and pride,
  Precocious now, yet precious in our view —
Strange, but not alien, bloom to love allied,
From treacherous blasts thy head empurpled hide,
  Rest till the season's truth evoke thy hue.

Anon when thy spring-tide spouse shall bid
    thee rise
In luteous veiling as a Roman bride,
When saffron beams shall meet thy sapphire
    dyes,
Blent in the iris of his affluent eyes,
    Vested in ambient Beauty's robes abide.

Linked then to glad florescent life assume
    Aurora's right to mark the Vernal hours,
The dawning of the roseate year relume
That weds the aureate to the floral bloom,
    The sun's affusions to thine azured flowers.

Rapt as Laconia in her love divine
    Our spring's oblation of thy praise shall be—
Her incense flooding Hyacinthus' shrine
Shall float in vibrant effluence to thine,
    Our pæans, O sun-wooed Hyacinth, to thee!

THE TEA-ROSE TRIAD.

ON A GIFT OF PRIZE ROSES FROM C. W. GALLOUPE, ESQ.

THREE roses rise envir'ning one gemmed
    view,
Dipped each in varying, yet enhancing, hue —
Steeped ever in a gleam of trinal Fancy's dew.

The Gontier's glow to rosy youth inclines,
The Bride, a maid's clear truth and trust en-
    twines —
The Mermet, with their loves in tint maternal
    shines.

A Child on ruby life of bloom is bending;
A Maiden, charms to pallid petals lending —
A Matron, ripe of grace, both traits and beau-
    ties blending.

TO THE GOLDEN ROD.

FLOWER that glad Summer gleams with
    charm indue,
   With conjuring rods evoking saffron dyes,
To vest nude hills in joy of hue,
To paint with cheer the vale's sad view
   And point above to freedom's sapphire skies —
Our Nation's beams now summon thee,
   For growth of liberty aglow to stand,
Her figured strength in bloom to be —
In garlands sun-wrought for the free,
   An aureate ensign on her golden land!

NYMPHŒA DEVONIENSIS.

(THE NIGHT-BLOOMING WATER LILY.)

NAIAD of flowers, now supine, yet not sleeping,
With petals 'neath half-parted sepals peeping,
Prone on the lake, and shy, till day's declining,
Hoarding pure dyes of pink through all its shining —
Not as the sirens of cerulean guise
That vaunt the sapphire of meridian skies —
That lure at noon — at night their jewels hide —
You spread vermilion cheer at eventide;
Claiming the charm of sunset's lingering glow —
Lovingly hold heaven's carmine beams below;
As if your kin of far-off Pharaoh's days
Had charged you 'gainst a term of banished rays

When space from last-lit rim to long-reft dome,
Should lapse to gloom of mural monochrome;
You gleam through soundless depths of wave
    and night
In symphonies of vibrant. florid light.

Whether of floral or fair human kind.
Nymph of sun-tinted form or love-hued mind,
Self-merged in storing joys for darkened hours
While halcyon sunshine woos the floating
    flowers;
For bloom like yours men's Fancy fragrant
    turns —
Grateful their frankincense of tribute burns!

CLOISTRAL AND MEMORIAL

Truth shines the brighter clad in
Verse.

POPE

THE HEROES OF MONTMARTRE.

[The birth of the Society of Jesus is traced to the vows made during a solemn visit at dawn, in 1534, of St. Ignatius, St. Francis Xavier, and their seven companions, to the crypt on Montmartre where Christian France for a thousand years has revered her martyr patron, St. Denys.]

LOOMING o'er Paris, grave Montmartre
    Heights
  Ages of wondrous deeds and themes recall:
Contests for Europe, strife for homeland rights,
    Pillaging Northman, struggling Rome and
    Gaul;
France on that Hill of Martyrs saw the doom
    Her soldier-god and her Apostle shared:
Napoleon, glory-crowned, engulfed in gloom;
    Denys confronting calm the fate he dared,
    Gaining in death the grander crown his life
    prepared.

This shrine of lustrous works saw one tran-
    scending,
    Outshining still its earthly glories' prime, —
A League for souls, a Heaven-sent Light por-
    tending
    Bright victory for millions through all time.
The darksome ante-dawn, a troublous year,
    Finds Clement dying, crushed by Papal
    care,
Switzer and Briton tempt the mad career
    And barter Faith of old for Esau's share, —
    But this Montmartre Sun lights up the dire
    despair.

Lo! from the shadow Notre Dame at dawn
    Throws down on waking Paris, come ascend-
    ing
The warrior souls from worldly paths withdrawn,
    Buoyant their way to gray Montmartre wend-
    ing,
Day-stars to light the mural future's sky,
    Toiling they long must climb —'tis Heaven's
    plan;

Full soon their lives for God shall fructify,
  And earth's elliptic orbit be the span
    Their toil shall reach, their victory for res-
    cued man.

With aspect martial and august, shines one
  Whose soul of fire was lit to gleam afar, —
Great Don Ignatius Gomez, Spain's blest son,
  Loyola's latest scion, Faith's last star;
Struck by the Power that stayed a Saul, and
  shook
Augustine's soul at Milan's school, this man
With Pampeluna's wounds and fame forsook
  Vain war and verse, and benisoned began
  Manresa's mighty Ode, — the theme, God's
  rights o'er man!

Beside him moves a youth whose spirit foun-
  tains
  O'erflowed with saving zeal a heathen strand;
Francis, the child of fair Navarra's mountains,
  "Angel of Indies," loved of every land;
To parched Japan he turned with Heavenly tide,

And washed, withal, her yield of faith's rich
    ore ;
But, like the land to Moses' feet denied,
    Harsh China left him spent on her bleak
        shore, —
    A wave receding, yet resounding evermore.

.   .   .   .

The germ such heroes planted bore the name,
    " Society of Jesus," — bore it far,
With fragrance blessing those who would de-
        fame,
    As sandal copse perfume the hands that mar.
Parara's banks record Arcadian days
    When   Jesuit   Mentors   showed   what   men
        might be ;
Huron and Kaffir, — all recite their praise,
    And all the flowing years in Time's drear sea
    Can never quench their fire or drown their
        memory.

TO A SISTER OF NOTRE DAME.

O SISTER parted, yet a sister still.
   Though claiming now a name we little
     knew.
Why take a trustful heart with steadfast will
   From those whom life's true tendons bind to you?
Vocation sweet allures you to your Lord,
   To find content in cloistered Notre Dame.
As mind and soul, conjoined in grand accord,
   Choose *Ad majorem Dei Gloriam.*

His greater glory now enshrines our pain,
   His mercy mitigation soft ensures.
His love may well your life and death enchain.
   Whose hallowed path and footprints now
     are yours.

Then as you yield to Him a soul sincere,
   Oft may your Patron yet the gift renew,
And by some grace of transmigration here,
   The Virgin Martyr live again in you.

Religion's gain lends grief of loss surcease —
   This choice of lot is but a happy haste;
Ours, sand oft swept by Passion's swift caprice,
   Yours, cool oasis midst a worldly waste.
O doubly Sister! that such claims entwine,
   What faithful light through doubtful years
     and dim,
To look toward one who yearns for Spouse
    Divine,
   And calmly leaves us evermore to cleave to
    Him!

A TRANSPLANTED BLOOM.

FROM every group Death takes a trophy
    dear,
  From every cluster claims a precious flower;
And now so soon he plucks you from us here,
    Bright friend of many a blithe and sunny
    hour.

How short it seems since last we happily met,
    With mingling mirth and friendship in each
    eye;
And while the thought with grief is struggling
    yet,
    How hard to give you but a prayer and last
    good-by!

O fresh and glad young life so early gone —
    O radiant mind and heart that still shall
      dwell
In loving prayer and memory, living on —
    We leave you with one tearful long farewell,
      farewell!

A MOTHER'S MEMORY.

PAST mortal change, yet cherished still,
　　O deep and deathless mother love,
Thy children stricken feel the thrill —
The living themes their memories fill —
　　Thy heart beats vibrant from above!

'Mid blest transition dear — not dead —
　　O passing soul, thou may'st not cease —
Abiding in a heavenly bed
May ever rest thy placid head —
　　Thy loving spirit sleep in Life of Peace!

A YOUNG HEART STRICKEN.

ON J. E. S.

HEAVEN now thy vital toil has stayed,
    Thy last faint pulsing tender stilled,
    Lifting — to prove thy task fulfilled —
The load of pain upon thee laid.

O fair young Heart so swiftly gone —
    O throbbing Life in sweet release,
    Passing through griefs to longed-for
      peace —
Thy beating vibrant lingers on!

Thy chords yet sounding none may sever —
    Their impulse blends bereaved heart's
      striving,
    In resonance of love surviving —
In living unison forever!

THE HIGHER VISION.

IN REPLY TO A DECLARATION OF ROBERT G. INGERSOLL.

"WE know not, live not, past this
    mundane sight"—
Proclaims a groper in Agnostic night;
Then must we limn in clay what men may
    know,
What lines his loftier visions claim below—
Must carnal bounded themes be deified,
Heaven's craved revealings to his Hope de-
    nied —
Life deemed a chain with fleshly links in-
    wrought,
The world a charnel house for soul-reft
    thought?

Look to that law set primal in his heart
Whose glow the pencilling rays Divine impart;
'Tis but in prostrate purpose, loth to rise,
'Tis with the prone of will the low view
    lies;
High-lit analogies the answer tell;
O'er torpid Nature fires resurgent dwell;
Dead bulbs as 'lumined lilies in such ray
Arise and breathe in Resurrection's day;
Numb chrysalis forms take iridescent wing;
Pent germs from prisoning orbs soar free and
    sing.

Is man more gross than bulb or grub or germ,
His essence — through all matters cycling
    term —
Less volatile than those of basest guise
That mount to ether, baffling corporal eyes?
His vaulting flame less alien to decay
Than sparks that out corrosion light their way,
While in their flash ethereal space is riven
And circumfusing arc spans earth and heaven?

Creation's universal voice replies.
Despite transition, psychic force ne'er dies —
Repels the phasma of a spirit-death —
Immortal essence spent with mortal breath;
Dispels Nirvana dreams of palsied rest,
Spurning their lethal peace for life possessed —
Telling that man shall see, his being shine
Beyond all cosmic spheres in light Divine
Living as everlasting ages roll
In higher sight — in holier vision of his Soul!

HYMNS

Fortunati ambo si quid mea
carmina possunt.

ÆNEID.

LET NOT THY FACE AVERTED BE.

L ET not Thy face averted be,
      Though ours for sin have swerved from
         Thee —
      Thy love, O Lord, unprized —
Nor turn with eyes upbraiding more,
But glance forgiving as before
      On hearts now agonized!

O beam benignant once again
On fleeting lives and wills of men
      In Passion's ruffling view —
Where murky waves in currents fierce
Repel faint lights that strive to pierce.
      May Thine come changeless through!

O face illumed of Olivet, shine —
Full in the radiance Divine
    Thy light transmuting pour —
That on dimmed souls Thy rays may rest,
As on Veronica's Veil impressed,
    Avert Thee nevermore!

O ESCA VIATORUM!

AFTER ST. THOMAS AQUINAS.

O FOOD of pilgrims faltering low!
    O Bread that angel hosts foreshow,
        O Manna from on high,
Thou givest taste of Heaven's own life
To stay the craving and the strife —
        Our faint hearts hungry cry!

O Font Divine — o'erflowing Love,
That out a Saviour's breast above,
        A rapturing current rolls —
Sweet to our sin-parched nature streaming,
O Living Spring from death redeeming
        Restore our swooning souls!

O Jesus, loved in light revealed —
Though now in guise of bread concealed
    Lie all supernal rays,
Grant that this veil withdrawn may be, —
Our eyes Thy risen glory see
    Transfixed in deathless gaze !

AVE MARIA.

PARAPHRASED FOR MUSICAL THEME ON BACH'S THIRD PRELUDE.

O LOVE inspiring —
    O Mary, grace possessed,
        Choice of all creatures blest,
Life of our souls desiring —

                        Ave Maria.

Hail thou in whom the Lord abides,
In whom maternal sway resides —
Man's wav'ring heart in thee confides —

                    Ave Maria!

Star most illuming,
    Send holiest rays
    Through sin-wrapped days,
Piercing their gloom — their grief consuming —

                    Ave Maria!

O Loving Beam, on sinners shine —
O Mother, lend this glow of thine,
Then light us to thy Son Divine —

> > > Ave Maria!
> > > Amen.

MISCELLANEOUS

Poetry is the music of thought conveyed to us in the music of language.

CHATFIELD.

THE MUSE OF ISRAEL.

MOURN not the Muse of Israel's children
        flown,
O Sons, that nigh her Wall of Wailing moan —
Deem not her tuneful day forever fled,
Her Cantors gone — their vibrant grandeur
        dead,
For Judah lives while Levi's Songs are sung,
Or love or grief from lyre of David wrung —
While captive chants o'er Babylon Waters'
        side —
As timbrels over Egypt's yawning Tide,
Plaintive in cadence of their long ago,
Enchain the soul with psalteries of woe!

Sweet through the Age's air she breathes
    again
The rhythmic charm by her bequeathed to
    men ;
And still her harp its theme harmonious brings,
Though ruthless hands essay to rend the
    strings ;
Rossini, Mendelssohn, and Meyerbeer —
With such her Genius fills the Century's
    ear ;
Her dulcet melody enchanting floats
On Pasta's wave — on Grisi's liquid notes —
On voiceful grace of ranks that resonant throng
To blend her chords of psalmody and song —
From joys that Miriam's jubilation rang
To sorrows Jephtha's daughter dolorous sang.

O Israel's marvelled Muse, what deathless power
Invests thy pensive life with vital dower —
Æolian harp hung o'er one race alone,
Whence is the breeze that wafts thy stayless
    tone ?

'Tis that which bore the Sire at Heaven's com-
 mand
Across Euphrates to thy hallowed Land,
His Spirit bids thee sad or buoyant be —
His Canticles of Zion sigh and sing through thee !

THE HARP OF MOORE.

WRITTEN FOR THE MOORE CENTENARY.

THE statue at Thebes, in the shade mute as
    doom,
  Gave musical strains when the morn-light
    shone o'er;
So the Nation, once silent as Memnon in
  gloom,
  Trilled forth tuneful plaints in the sunshine
    of Moore.

His verse lent the rays that relumine her glory,
  His lyrics the voice still reciting her praise;
And their heart-thrilling themes yet revive her
    gone story —
  Her mirth and her melody live in his lays.

An Æolian harp on a banyan bough pending,
  His Muse and sweet numbers were wafted
    above;
But his soul, to the soil, like the banyan tree
    bending
  Bore her best notes again to the Isle of his
    love.

'Twas no monochord music he rendered alone,
  For each lyre-string sang her renown and her
    wrong:
Famed Amphion raised Thebes by his harp's
    magic tone —
  Moore exalted the land by the spell of his
    song.

OLIVER WENDELL HOLMES.

GENIUS of dual flame by Nature lit,
　　With twin-borne lights of poesy and wit,
Whose pencilled beams in threads of thought
　　intwine,
And clear through fourscore years of veiling
　　shine,
The century's old — a decade sole remains —
Our autocrat in Fancy's youth still reigns;
The virile verse reveals no swerving rays —
The poise of theme no senile lapse betrays.

Share long the glow of lines that shall not die,
Their sparkle's living reflex in your eye —
Chastened as diamond facets, keen and pure,
Fashioned alike to glisten and endure;

Your vital lamp in iridescence burning,
Changing consummate tints with every turn-
    ing —
Ever with incandescent gleam illuming,
Kindling men's souls, yet ne'er itself consum-
    ing.

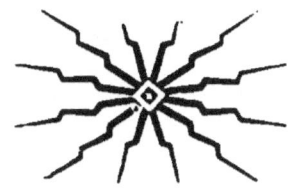

A VIRGILIAN CHARADE.[1]

A LATIN term in my full form is traced,
　　Whose primal part the hero's claim as-
sumes —
A clear enclitic in my last is placed,
　　Linking a theme that Virgil's soul consumes
With life of deeds by Classic Art unrolled,
　　To light whose name the epic fire he brings —
A man set forth in his exalted mould,
　　Whose fame in sweet hexameters he sings.

---

[1] *Answer:* The word *virumque*, from the first line of the Æneid.

THE SACRED WHITE ELEPHANT FROM SIAM.

[Written in response to an offer by P. T. Barnum. — The White Elephant of Siam has been held sacred to Guatama in the religion of the Buddhists, and called by the people Toung Taloung.]

OUT from the Orient. — auric home pri-
    meval. —
Realm of the unreal — maze of mythic lore. —
From palmy clime, with primal day coeval,
    Earth's peering oriel where her dawn-rays
      pour !

First to the Occident — from mystic thrall
    Is lent the light of Thai's faith and throne,
The aulic elephant of Siam's lustral hall.
    In guise that great Guatama claims alone.

Sacred Leviathan of land renowned —
  Chosen of Buddha — Rose of vernal shrine
A myriad chants on Ava's magic ground
  Bespeak the claims of Toung Taloung divine.

Behind his hallowed stamp of hue revealed,
  Centuple tongues their mysteries have told,
A chiliad of visioned deeds unsealed,
  A thousand lustrums' vanished dreams un-
    rolled.

'Round Toung Taloung, like Indra's censers
    swung,
  Cycles of Buddha sweep in weird progres-
    sion, —
Their incense breathes as lays on Meinam sung
  Of memories chimed in rhythmic retrocession.

THE LAST DAY OF POMPEII.

AUGUST 24, A.D. 79.

WIDESPREAD the centuries, like cinders
    down Vesuvia's side,
Have passed o'er dead Pompeii since that last,
    that fatal tide
Of flame and livid lava fell, enfolding thick in
    gloom
Her homes, her pomp, her stricken site in one
    vast living tomb.

Festive the day broke over broad Campania's
    plain and town,
And even grim Vesuvius' brow for once forgot
    to frown,
While all encircling hills exulted in the morn-
    ing's breath,
When doomed Pompeii's people thronged to
    glut their eyes on death.

Her gaudy villas smiled above the mist and
  valley then,
Her red-tiled roofs and time-worn towers rose
  young and gay again;
Forum and stately arch of triumph shadowed
  naught of strife —
Portal and crowning statue greeted laden streams
  of life.

Stay! for despite their joy the prescient Pliny,
  wise as brave,
Foreboding, marks the trembling shore repel the
  tardy wave,
And listening, hears with soul of awe, the mur-
  mur hoarse and deep
Along the beauteous river's bank and laughing
  meadow creep!

"The gods protect the guiltless! vengeful Orcus
  bursts with ire!" —
Swift the velaria tent reveals the Mountain's
  rav'nous fire;

The gladiator, quivering low, is left to rise or
    die —
Lions athirst for life now turn, with human
    fear, to fly.

Night o'er the realm of Noon with rushing
    blackness swoops on all,
Vesuvia's vapor, shaped like pine trees, spread-
    ing as a pall;
In vain the priest of Isis craves to light the
    sacred flame,
Vainly the guard of Rome is nerved to body
    forth her name.

The late Gomorrah, as the old, in ashes sinks
    at last —
Her day is come, her doom is sealed, — her
    living power is past,
And yet exhumed Pompeii lives again to tell
    her story —
Clearer than Pliny's classic page to light her
    age and glory.

Thus oft o'erpowering fate that seems to leave
the heart forlorn

Serves but to save the thought and worth for
ages yet unborn,

As still survives and speaks above her ashes
and her woe

The city burned and buried eighteen hundred
years ago.

THE SOLITARY.

ON A PAINTING BY THE LATE BRADFORD FREEMAN — A
SOLITARY HERON IN A FOREST AT NIGHT.

NIGHT on the German wood — stillness and
    shade
  On plant, and leaf, save where bent linden
    trees
Receive the pensive moon-glance on the glade
  And nod their heads beneath the lulling
    breeze.

Now from his hermit home the heron steals —
  Mute peering watcher, solemn vigil keeping;
Sullen and lone, strange longing he reveals
  To muse on night and sombre Nature sleep-
    ing.

Broods he again on Scandinavia's Land,
　On visits gone, or summers long ago,
Reviving joys that with the past expand,
　Or finding now alone the gloom of woe?

Thus hearts bereft of all love craved to see,
　Like hermit watchers 'mid a shrouded scene
Withdraw from themes that live or e'er may be,
　To dwell enwrapped with dreams of what
　　have been.

ON A GOLDEN WEDDING.

TO AMOS C. CLAPP.

OLD friend, the cycle of whose nuptial round
Has turned the golden matrimonial bound;

Five decades' mint now stamp your metal true,
Five generations sterling gleam in you.

Let not the wedlock's day be deemed declining,
Through which this golden sheen of lives is
    shining.

How few upon such gilded heights may meet,
How many seek them vain with faltering feet!

Too rare again their wedding bells are rung,
Too faint their notes for yours to lapse unsung.

What treasured thoughts these fifty years un-
    seal —
What freighted themes their lifted veils reveal!

Tried in the crucible that ever glows,
In time your life connubial brighter grows;

For you and her who shares we ask yet more —
The plaudits of our hearts bespeak encore.

May she and you shine on as burnished gold
    endures —
May benisons of years as bright be hers and
    yours.

A BOY'S CHRISTMAS GREETING.

LINES ENCLOSED WITH A PORTRAIT OF ADELBERT POTTER.

IN this — while children's Christmas songs are
    sung —
Receive the token of a loving boy,
Who, with his hope so fair and life so young —
His New Year's bells not yet five chimings
    rung —
    Would join in all your chanted season's joy.

Now, as the old year with glad greetings ends,
    To you, who may this modest likeness see,
His heart its message, as to kindliest friends,
To speak good cheer and banish sadness, sends —
    Let this your Adelbert's true keepsake be.

DUTY'S WEAR.

ON WILLIAM H. BALDWIN'S BIRTHDAY.

NOT rusting ease, but duty's wear, is
    blest —
The proverb of man's wasting day declares —
Here labors one who scorns corroding rest,
Whose works attuned in brain and heart attest
    His stayless nature neither rusts nor wears.

Like tapers buoyed, in clear unceasing glow,
    In limpid fluid pendant at a shrine,
His buoyant deeds unresting radiance show,
With beams above and grateful oil below
    Wherein the lights at once may float and
    shine.

Long may his lamp of life in bright emission
   Its benison to the shrine of youth bequeath,
A genial oil relieving heart attrition,
While effluent flame relumes each dimmed con-
    dition —
   Fed by his flow of kindliness beneath.

WEALTH AND WORTH.

ON THE LATE HENRY P. KIDDER.

AVER not now — "wealth evermore is cold,
  Incisive will enforcing icy heart,
While Crœsus' grasp imposes gyves with
  gold " —
Here gleamed a heart whose affluent rays could
  hold
    Such wealth of warmth as souls aglow impart;
    A will of olden flame for civic weal,
That burned at wrong, yet beamed with hope
    on woe ;
A life of worth that homes of pain reveal,
Uplifting deeds he veiled in loving zeal —
    The grief, the gloom of loss abide below.

JOHN BOYLE O'REILLY.

LOST to men's eyes, the beams so loving given
Of him by whose life's rending ours was riven —
The virile brain, suffused in blazoned light,
Turned swift from flush of noon to shroud of night,
The heart, whose cords we dreamt no fate should sever,
Torn now from vibrant touch of ours forever!
Can we believe this throbbing Nature dead —
Speak the cold word that notes a spirit fled?

That is too dark in prosy gloom — too drear —
For chosen son of Poesy and Cheer.
Earth's veil no more his radiance conceals —
This rent his full-orbed being's ray reveals,
With rounded gleam that conjures to our
    gaze
His diorama wrought of 'lumined days.

To goal of loftiest dream a hero bends
And sings a martial strain as he ascends:
Anigh the summit's steep the youth arrives,
Fronted with gibbets — bound with felons'
    gyves:
For patriot crime that despot ne'er condoned,
Sent forth as one dishonored and disowned —
A lot that never e'en the solace gave
To kneel above a grief-spent mother's grave.

Though exile fate weighed sore on thought and
    will —
The poet's proud soul rose, unfettered still:

In harshest realms new scenes of beauty
    learned,
New lessons charged with heaven-hued love dis-
    cerned ;
And yet not all that fancy deemed most good —
Banyan, nor banksia glade, nor Austral wood,
Jungle of India, — flora of Cathay —
Not gorgeous South, nor " Land of the Malay,"
Nor Java slumbering in her yellow air
Could ever, for his filial eyes, compare
With that lost Motherland, in plaint, so sweet,
Whose face his life was nevermore to meet.

But now that life, denied to Old World view,
Was lit to shine in iris of the New,
Twin hemispheres in vision to embrace,
With arching bow to span each storm-bent
    race.
Here were his Nature's wide refracted beams
To shed divergent yet concentred gleams
As diamond facets rival glintings show
While all are blent in iridescent glow.

O friend, who from the hour you touched this
    Western land,
Has held our captive heart-strings in your hand,
You wove our loves in one — proving with voice
    and pen
What life-spun web a man may spread for
    men,
Knit with the threads of sympathy that bind —
The interlacing ties that link mankind!

A LIFE'S LOVE SONG.

TO M. O'M.

AS the sun-beams with amber tinge shine
  Through the sheaves that responsive are
glowing,
Thy heart lends a glad hue to mine,
  In Love's golden bloom ever growing.

Thy radiance with Love's ripening powers,
  In the gleam of warm glances alluring,
Endows me with fruitage and flowers
  Of a sweetness and fragrance enduring.

O Love, may thy vital rays glow
  Like the sun-beams their saffron diffusing —
All thy tints on my being bestow,
  My life-growths forever suffusing !

TO CONVALESCENCE.

A SONNET.

FREE from a thrall of peril and of pain —
　　A vale of grieving and unstayed suspense,
Of pang convulsive and nerve-pulsing tense —
The sufferer comes at last to thy domain,
O nurse-like Convalescence, to regain
　　Between Death's aim and lusty Life's defence,
　　The tranquil moods that thy calm powers dis-
　　　　pense —
To claim again the balm of placid brain,
　　Plucked from the fever throes like burning
　　　　brand,
To feel the chastened thought thy ways instil,
　　And turn from vaunted strength to His great
　　　　hand,
Who holds each mortal throb — each vital
　　　　thrill —
　　Within all-mastering touch of His command,
As threads that vibrate with His sway of will!

RONDEAU TO HEALTH.

HAIL peerless Health, ordained with life
    decree,
The vital sun of mortal day to be —
   Apart from thee men's spheres their glow
    maintain —
   Glad cycles roll, their joys revolve in vain !
Touched by thy beam chill Nature sings with
    glee,
While lumined scenes of earth and air and sea,
In harmonies of cheery tone agree,
   And join in grateful chant with one refrain —
      Hail peerless Health !
Pent hearts from pris'ning weakness breaking
    free,
In light of thine find their releasing key;
   Reft of thy gleam no rays for man remain
   Save those that hallowed shine for Heavenly
    gain,
And priceless pay alone for loss of thee —
      Hail peerless Health !

CONSECRATION OF A BISHOP.

IN echoing chancel, arch and apse and choir,
For one bright soul what doth this impulse
  mean
That chant and stately liturgy inspire —
  "Move thou in care, in heart and station
    higher,"
For him is all the summons of the scene!

RONDEAU TO HEALTH.

HAIL peerless Health, ordained with life
     decree,
The vital sun of mortal day to be —
    Apart from thee men's spheres their glow
      maintain —
    Glad cycles roll, their joys revolve in vain!
Touched by thy beam chill Nature sings with
     glee,
While lumined scenes of earth and air and sea,
In harmonies of cheery tone agree,
    And join in grateful chant with one refrain —
        Hail peerless Health!
Pent hearts from pris'ning weakness breaking
     free,
In light of thine find their releasing key;
    Reft of thy gleam no rays for man remain
    Save those that hallowed shine for Heavenly
      gain,
And priceless pay alone for loss of thee —
        Hail peerless Health!

CONSECRATION OF A BISHOP.

IN echoing chancel, arch and apse and choir,
　For one bright soul what doth this impulse
　　mean

That chant and stately liturgy inspire —
　"Move thou in care, in heart and station
　　higher,"
　For him is all the summons of the scene!

FLOWERING YEARS.

ACCOMPANYING A GIFT OF NINE ROSEBUDS FROM A CLASSMATE,
TO MARION FULLER ON HER NINTH BIRTHDAY.

CLASSMATE, as in young bloom of budding
    day,
  Your life of flowering years has yielded nine;
I come with buds your claims of love to pay, —
  For every full-blown year indite a line,
  With hope that in these tiny gifts of mine,
To each fair calyx friendship's hue may cling,
  And rosy joys in every petal twine, —
On MARION's birthdays flowers of bliss to fling,
On each fair bloss'ming Fuller fragrance bring.

A VANISHED RAY.

HEAVEN lent our lives one cheery ray —
   One tinge of dawn to lure our sight
As prelude of a love-lit day,
Whose tint no cloud should bear away —
  Then turned its radiance to Bereavement's
    night.

But yet thy nature's morn is bright —
   O tender gleam, not darkly gone,
For thou hast winged thine infant flight
To give back glory of maturer light —
  Sweet baby Soul forever beaming on!

A brief and broken ray no more,
   Pure little Life in memory shine —
May glow from glad celestial shore
Thy being's rosy dawn restore —
  Relumined envoy of a day divine!

A WEDDING GREETING.

LIKE the linking of word and fit thought —
　　The wedding of phrase and of feeling,
In sweet lyrics that poets have wrought —
　　Kin beauties responsive revealing.
The blending of hearts joined as yours
　　In a life that on wedlock reposes
Love and bliss in each full sphere insures,
　　And their two-fold enhancing discloses.

ON A COMPOSER'S WEDDING.

WITH nuptial tones to discord ne'er de-
    scending,
In union may your notes and lives be found,
Connubial bliss with bridal music blending
In unison of melodies unending —
    Love's antiphons from heart to heart re-
    sound;
To loftier harmonies of hopes attain,
    And as your chant of life hymeneal rolls,
May hymns of concord rise in chiming strain —
Earth's joy-rung chords attuned to Heaven's
    refrain,
    In symphony of love-concerted souls.

HARRY M'GLENEN'S BIRTHDAY.

A S some fair hill by Autumn's fruit o'er
grown,
While Summer lingers, seeming loth to part,
Good friend, though life's autumnal blasts have
blown,
And round your head the dark-winged years
have flown,
Your nature basks in sunshine of the heart;
Long in its ray aglow with fruit abound,
While birthday joy a gladdening garland
weaves—
May foliage of loves entwined be found,
That Winter's blanching eyes may see you
crowned
With Friendship's wreath of glorious tinted
leaves.

COLUMBIA THEATRE, BOSTON.

TEMPLE new-graced within our Drama's
pale,
Our histrion greeting sings "Columbia, Hail!"
Welcome to speak through deep theatric theme —
To realize the high dramatic dream.
Enlisting native thought upon the stage,
To share the playwright's laurels of the age —
To sound the claims of this new Thespian day,
And voice the blended charms of Thalia's sway!

"THE COUNTY FAIR."

LIKE the breeze from a meadow of newly-
　　mown hay —
　Like the tinkling of bells — the far lowing of
　　kine —
Come the scenes that this drama's clear outlines
　　portray,
The sounds blent with themes of the quaint and
　　the gay,
　Where the breaths of wild blossoms and wood-
　　lands combine.

They come with allurements of sweet rural air,
　That give fragrance to joys and a freshness to
　　charm
Of the glees and the dances and drolleries there —
Of the glad Husking Bee and the famed County
　　Fair —
　And kindly Aunt Abby on Rockbottom Farm.

Too radiant and rare are such growths of the
    scene —
Too flowerless our natures and sterile our age,
That fruitage so glowing, with fancies so green,
Should fail ere our mem'ries can garner and glean
    Or fade where they stand on the field of our
    stage.

With force that whirls the letter-face so fast,
Faust, Schöffer — Gutenberg — would gaze aghast,
For these gone fathers of the Art Preservative
Would fear us lost to all their paths conserva-
    tive.

But our new product's claims are not confined
To merits touching a mechanic's mind —
Ever must roll of speediest press be vain
Apart from swifter press-work of the brain;
With that each quickened day's revolving wheel
Its quota of revival will reveal —
With that our full rejuvenated "Journal,"
Pressing, in this régime, her round diurnal,
A vital pledge for her new quarto holds
In life infused that every leaf enfolds,
And thus without duplicity presages
A duplication of her progress as her pages.

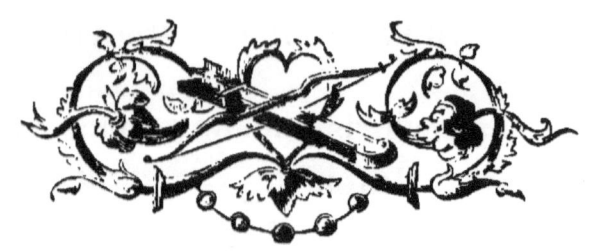

THE WAR SONGS.

O SONGS of the War, you resound for us ever
　　With chantings of glory that cannot decay—
Our lives and our heroes the years swiftly sever,
But yours is a grandeur that lives on forever—
　　Though born amid death you shall ne'er die
　　away!

ODE TO OUR NAVAL HEROES.

WRITTEN AT THE INVITATION OF THE CITY OF BOSTON, AND
SUNG AT THE ADMIRAL PORTER MEMORIAL
SERVICE, MAY 14, 1891.

O VICTORS of war and of wave —
Themes that live in loved vision to-day —
Our song rings of valor and life-drops you
gave,
Our pæans in glory repay;
Again with array of their pride,
Your Argosies burst on our view.
To tower above Treason and foes of the Tide,
To blaze for a Nation anew!

Not with navies in grim palisade,
Nor hordes in Armadas hurled,
But with armor of Freedom firm guard is made,
From our gateways, to ward off a world;
In War's chafings of sea and of strand
Your Knighthood our honor shall keep;
In their challenge of wrath and of strife to
our Land,
The brave duel shall dare on the deep.

Your Record to time shall not yield,
  Bright emblazoned on river and main,
With those deeds for the flag shown on deck
      and on field,
  That defied aught of rending or stain.
    As great billows now swell, — now are
      gone, —
      Pealing long on their reach to the shore,
    Your life-forms recede, but your fame surges
      on,
      And in memory resounds evermore.

O Land fused in Liberty's fire,
  Whose heroes are lit in thy flame,
Our thought with the pulsing their heart-throbs
      inspire,
  Is kindled in chanting thy name;
    Our tributes aglow to each son,
      With a soul that burned filial and free —
    For the triumphs he wrought, for the
      trophies he won —
      Are rolled up in praise sung to thee!